U Got Next I Got Now

Stop Living Your Life Like It's A Rehearsal;
This Is The Only One You Get

Melvin Anthony Bethea

Dedication

I dedicate this book to anyone around the world who was told they would not be succeeding at anything in life. This book is for the underdogs, for the people who are rejected by society. I'm here to let you know that you are born to win, so do not condition yourself to lose. God has given everyone a special gift to give to the world; do not sit and say you have nothing. The world is starving for greatness. If you fall down nine times, get up the tenth time to benefit yourself and others. This is the only life you get.

Acknowledgment

I want to thank GOD because, without His love, I am nothing. To my oldest daughter, Taylor Romel Bethea. From the first time the nurse placed you in my arm, I knew I would meet death before I would let you meet harm. You showed me how to truly love the human race, and for that, I will always be grateful. You know your dad loves you. To my middle daughter, Dominique Riley, I love you very much, and I pray one day, we will get to re-meet each other. And to my baby girl, Maddison L. Bethea. You are your own little person. I love you to the moon and back.

You make me a better man. To my big sister, Shelly, you are the best sister a man can ask for. You have saved me so many times. You're God sent. I truly love you. To my grandparents, Bernice Thomas, Clarence (Sam) Thomas, and My Big Mama, Catherine Johnson. I thank you for taking a broken 14-year-old boy and raising me into a man. Thank you for loving me when I could not find love for myself. Thank you for teaching me that God loves me even if I'm not perfect. I have so much to thank you for. To my parents, Catherine Johnson and Melvin Bethea, thank you.

About the Author

Melvin Anthony Bethea is a GOD fearing man, father, son, and friend. Melvin got his professional start in the District and the Federal government. In Human Capital Management, Melvin has worked with such agencies as DOD, TSA, FEMA, DOL, FDA, FBI, OPM, HHS, and the SEC. Melvin's true love is real estate and stock market. He believes that everybody on earth has a gift to give to the world. A large part of being a good leader is making decisions-but how often do we stop and think about our own decision-making process. Melvin Anthony Bethea.

Preface

Most people dream of navigating through their life successfully; however, only a few of them really know how to turn their dream into reality. They want to figure it all out but often find themselves lost with no direction to set their path. This book talks about what such people are missing and where they are lagging. It holds a set of noteworthy guidelines as to what everyone must know and live by. You don't become successful overnight without partaking in constant endeavors to become better equipped in dealing with challenges life throws at your door. Everything needs consistency, determination, efforts, and strategy. This book will teach you how you can win and succeed by following some strategies that I guarantee you will swear by your entire life.

Contents

Chapter 1
Time

Time is one of the most-used nouns in the English language, yet it remains a mystery. Time is an incredibly valuable resource - a commodity that everyone has in equal amounts. The day has got 24 hours, yet everybody uses that time in their own way. They achieve less or more depending on how proactively the time given to them is spent.

Whatever happens over the course of time is irreversible. If we have to spend it against our liking or things do not flow the way we expected them to, nothing can be undone. This is the best quality of time. It never stops. Everything on this earth can stop for one reason or the other but time is a continuous process. So, if you're going through tough times or even good ones for that matter, remember it would not stay this way forever. The clock is always ticking. This can be your motivation to strive to work well or your hope that no matter how uncertain life seems, days and nights will continuously change. Come what may, every morning can be better than the previous one.

However, we seem to achieve less than more, getting so little of time. It does not matter who you are. From Bill Gates to Oprah Winfrey, or even a regular guy like me, i.e., Melvin Anthony Bethea, gets the same amount of time each day. So, why do some people achieve more while others achieve less with the time they have? The problem is not with the amount of time but what we do with it. Take a look at some of the world's highly productive people, and you will notice some critical details.

How these people spend their time from sunup to sundown is very different from how people usually spend their time. Besides, these people keep certain points close to their hearts. For example, those who are productive always stay focused. They have the concept of effective time management down to a science, have goals, and diligently strive when it comes to achieving them.

Successful and productive people seem to always be in a rush; in fact, the ones I have come into contact with are always conscious of their time. They hate wasting time. Every minute counts for them just as it should!

"Time is what we want the most, but what we use the worst" -**William Penn.**

There indeed are very few of us who know the value of time. They say 'time is money' for a reason. It is because, just like money, you can spend it on the right things to gain present or future value. Another reason time has monetary value is that once spent, it does not come back. It depreciates. Time is the one commodity you can never get back. Is there any way to manage time effectively and get all the things done that you want to do or achieve? Therefore, it is crucial to manage your time wisely as you take on the journey to reach your chosen end-goal.

The idea that time is money, however, is highly debatable to some and is still questioned. While time and money share a lot of characteristics, the former is a lot more important. This is why we must not waste time and not let others waste it as well.

"Time is a gift that most of us take for granted" **-Cheryl Richardson**

The sad matter is that we only take out time for what we believe is important, which can be both important or unimportant. We tangle ourselves so deeply in situations that waste our time that we forget to take out time for the things that really matter. Our goals and aspirations are left in the backseat, giving way to procrastination and having an unclear direction. Time management is an art that experts need to learn, especially those who have every minute of their day planned out and follow the schedule religiously. There are a few points that commoners can learn from their example, which are:

- Do not let situations waste your time.
- Focus on the time you have.
- Focus on the goal you want to accomplish.

Time waits for no one; that's one detail that you must remember.

Better Time Management Means Better Productivity

"The bad news is time flies... the good news is you are the pilot" -Michael Altshuler

Often, we look at famous people who get things done and reach all of their goals, thinking, 'why cannot we be in the same boat?' We look at them and wonder why they are ahead in life and so successful. Is it because they are just better than us? Or is it because they have something that we do not? The answer to both these questions is a loud, resounding 'no.' It is not that those people are better or they have something that we do not; it is just that they can manage their time better. It goes without saying that expecting good results and achieving goals without putting in the effort is a mere fantasy. Constant practice and effort, along with effective time management skills, are essential. As it is said, 'practice makes perfect.' We need to practice and hone our craft by putting in the necessary time.

It is just like learning a technical skill - you would not become good at it if an adequate amount of time is not invested. Similarly, you would not be to achieve your goals or become successful without putting in the time that is needed. Be honest and ask yourself these questions: 'Am I using my time wisely? Am I using my time to the best of my ability?'

Before I got set on the right path in time management, I wasted a lot of time. In the past, I was guilty of being a chronic procrastinator. I wasted a lot of my time on foolishness. From watching TV and socializing excessively to spending hard-earned money that I got after dedicating a reasonable amount of time, I did everything to waste my time. All of these things gave me joy at the moment, but they were a waste of my time. They were taking away time that I could use to focus on and achieve my goal. If you are wasting your time, get yourself centered, and refocused. I'll give you three tips on getting yourself focused.

One - Wake up early in the morning, and pray or meditate. No one who says, "I'm not a morning person" is right. When you're passionate about your goal, you go the extra mile and become what you need to become.

Two - Cut out leisurely activities and stay focused on the path that lies in front of you.

Three - Stay away from people and situations that waste your time.

I cannot convey to you how precious your time is. Each minute that goes by in your life is time off of your life. Each time that you do not use your time wisely, or are unable to use it to help others, it's wasted. I get amazed when I watch athletes and entertainers who excel at a high level. Take Floyd Mayweather, for example. I look at his work ethic and how much time he puts in the gym, working out. You cannot get to stay on top for close to 20 years without putting in this time. I look at Sean Combs (a.k.a. Puff Daddy), Shawn

Carter(a.k.a. Jay-Z), Madonna, Prince Mohammed Ali, and the list goes on. These are all highly successful people that have a great work ethic requiring them to put in a lot of time. Learning how to manage your time is not an easy task. You're going to have to unlearn a lot of bad habits. This can be done depending on how dedicated you are to your goal. Only I know in my transition from this behavior. I did not realize how many bad time management habits I had developed over the years. It is only with patience, persistence, and practice, however, that your time management skills can get better.

What do Successful People do with Their Time?

"People of accomplishment rarely sat back and let things happen to them. They went out and happened to things." - **Leonardo da Vinci.**

Did Winston Churchill, Nelson Mandela, and Steve Jobs have more time every day than us? Of course, not. They just knew how to manage their time. After all, making time is easy, and in the end, it is all about time management. The highly successful people that we hear about do not wait and hope for the desired results. Success is never accidental to them. Are you wondering what it means? It is just that the success these people enjoy is the direct result of preparing, planning, and aligning their time with their most important goals and aspirations. If you do not value time, it does not value you back. This is the statement every successful man gives because if they had given little importance to time, they would not have been able to achieve their goals. Time is a resource everyone shares equally, but not all of us utilize it usefully.

The pattern our lives partake is dependent on the time spent. Successful intellectuals prioritize time. And time prioritization is based on firstly, identification of what is important to us, and secondly, time allocations. If you do not know where your time should be going, you would not be where you want to be, either. Just how the waves of the sea can never be made stagnant, so is the case with time. What we can only do is control its flow.

Following are eight ways in which successful people make the most of the time that they have:

They Save Their Decision Making Muscles for Important Stuff

It is unwise to worry about little things that do not even matter. While in office, former president of the United States, Barack Obama, only wore blue or gray suits. Zuckerberg's uniform is a gray shirt and jeans. Steve Jobs used to wear only blue jeans and a black turtleneck almost every day.

What can we derive from this information? It is better to simplify the things that can be simplified, for example, our wardrobe, to keep ourselves from wasting a lot of time on this useless thing. Successful people minimize the number of decisions they make on trivial matters. If we think about it, spending so much time on what we'll wear for the day wastes precious minutes that could be spent doing something else and much better.

Simply put, some seemingly unrelated and petty decisions truly matter when it comes to managing time. Successful people have internalized that every decision does not have to be optimal or perfect. This, in turn, frees them to make quick decisions most of the time. In effect, they automate and simplify decisions.

They do not spend time thinking about the little stuff like going to the gym or not. They do not make a deliberate effort to plan what they will have for breakfast. They work out at the same time every day and eat the same breakfast every day. They use their willpower and flex their decision-making muscles on the highest impact decisions they face every day and not ones that would not leave an impact on their lives. Cutting it short, minimizing the choices you have in life is an excellent way to manage time better.

They Have a Constant Morning Routine

There are many reasons to wake up every morning and follow the same routine. For starters, momentum is created at the start of the day by following a consistent and positive morning routine. What is the best combination of activities that successful people implement in their morning routine?

- Meditation
- Reading
- Writing a journal
- Exercising
- Prioritizing their day-to-day activities
- Envisioning a successful day

- Eating a nutritious breakfast to fuel their day

For example, motivational speaker Tony Robbins takes a cold shower every morning to rest his system and reduce inflammation. He also does breathing exercises and expresses gratitude during a ten-minute priming exercise. Through his morning routine, he chooses to expand gratefulness over fear and anxiety, seeing how our mind develops whatever we focus on.

A precise formula that produces a productive morning routine does not exist. It is different for everyone. This is why highly successful people experiment with various activities until they find the perfect morning routine that fits their lifestyle and sets them up for a successful day.

They Have a Consistent Nightly Routine

"Before anything else, preparation is the key to success"
-Alexander Graham Bell.

The thing about successful people is that they do not wait until the morning to prepare for a successful day. They start the night before! What do they do? Successful people recognize the importance of having an undisturbed, good night's sleep. So, they unplug from their devices, read, meditate, and plan for the next day. As a result, they wake up relaxed and stress-free because they have already designed the blueprint for having a productive day! However, they not only spend some part of the night (before going to sleep), planning for the next day, but they do it well!

They Plan Thoroughly

*"Give me six hours to chop down a tree, and I will spend the first four sharpening the axe." -**Abraham Lincoln.***

One of the major differences between highly successful people and average performers is the effort put into the planning stage. Successful people focus on detailed and strategic planning. In fact, they spend more time thinking about their big picture goals and ideas. They zoom out regularly to analyze their lives from a 50,000 ft. view. How does this help?

It helps in the manner that they are able to make key decisions deliberately, methodically, and strategically. Average performers make the same decisions in a reactive mode, while they are in the thick of the forest of their lives. They get to enjoy lesser rewards for their laborers at odd timings, whereas successful people plan thoroughly and reap the rewards consistently down the road. Their detailed planning provides clarity on what they should be working on at any given time. They produce at high levels because they separate the planning and creation processes., which means they do not just plan when they feel like it.

They Have a System for Planning

While Bill Gates was still the chairman at Microsoft, he used to seclude himself from the distractions of daily life during Think Week. This was an event that took place twice every year. Visitors were banned during the week, and he spent that time reading papers about Microsoft as well as new ideas in technology during this one week. This exercise allowed him to take a step back to review the projects and ideas at Microsoft.

It is also a good idea to conduct a review to define the most critical objectives for the following three months. What does not get scheduled, would not get done. It is a simple fact. Successful people regularly schedule a time to monitor their progress on key objectives and iterate their plans based on results and lessons learned. They make it a point to schedule their projects on a daily and weekly basis, setting time aside to not only plan but also to execute those plans.

They Work On the Most Important Project First

Successful people recognize that willpower is a limited resource that depletes as we make decisions, run errands, and work on various tasks and projects throughout the day. A full tank of willpower is effectively used and leveraged in the morning, by working on the most important project first.

They do not clutter their minds just as they wake up in the morning with the stresses and obstacles that could arise throughout the day. They take advantage of their fresh and clear mind. Besides, they take advantage of the lack of distractions in the early morning. They get a head start on the world by making progress towards their most valued goal in the morning.

Imagine this scenario: There is a bank that credits your account each morning with $86,400. The account carries over no balance from day-to-day transactions. Every evening, it deletes whatever part of the balance was not used during that day. Now, what would you do? You draw out every cent. Think about it, assuming that each one of us has such a bank called time. Every morning, this bank credits our account with 86,400 seconds and writes off the unused or wasted seconds that were not invested wisely. This process carries no balance and no overdraft.

Each day, it opens a new account for you. If you fail to use the day's deposit, the loss is yours. There is no going back. There is no drawing against tomorrow. You must live in the present on today's deposit. Invest it in every opportunity. The clock is running. You've got to make the most of today right here, right now.

Another thing to remember is that.

'Time waits for no one.'

Make every second count because you only get a fixed amount of time in a day. Whatever remains will get erased the next day. Follow up on every lead. Always get to the closing and remember that every opportunity missed equals money lost.

"Yesterday is history, tomorrow is a mystery, but today is a gift. That is why it is called the present" – Master Oogway.

Want to know the importance of time?

- Ask a student who failed a grade

about the value of a year

- Ask a mother who gave birth to a premature baby about the value of a month
- Ask the editor of a weekly newspaper about the value of a week
- Ask someone who missed

the train by a minute about the value that every minute holds in our lives

- Ask a person who avoided an accident with the gap of nanoseconds about the value of the seconds that tick by unnoticed
- Ask the value of one millisecond from a person who got the silver medal at the Olympics

Put yourself in the above-given people's shoes and think about what could happen in seconds, minutes, hours, and days that they could not catch-up on.

How to Combat Time

Organize. If you are like most people who sleep six to eight hours per day, leaving you somewhere between sixteen to eighteen hours left to earn, you will quickly realize the role that time plays. The clock is running continuously. It will not stop regardless of whether you sleep for hours or forever.

- Set your calendar. Hold yourself accountable for EVERYTHING, including your sleep routine and the time you spend in the gym, on travel, personal tasks, work tasks, calls, meetings, reading, and training, etc.

- This may be the first time realizing how critical your time is, and it may scare you once broken down. Overcome this, and you will soon be able to accomplish more than ever before.

- Hold yourself accountable. It's easy to push things onto the next day. Now is not the time for everything. It's about time you start valuing every moment in your life and make it countable. Your mindset needs to change and be immersed in making the most out of every second. Share your calendar with others. Let them know what they can aspire to do. Hit every objective. Exceed expectations.

- You will soon begin to realize the value of sleep compared to time. Six to eight hours? Time is winning, not you. It's time to take control. Cut out the nonsense.

Sooner or later, you will get a certain level of understanding about time. It can and will get crazy. Understand what you are willing to sacrifice vs. accomplish and plan accordingly. Remember, taking out time for the things you love doing should be easy. If you do not take out time for yourself, who will?

Nonetheless, amid all this struggle, happiness and peace of mind are to be kept constant. Achieving your goals will indeed make you happy but spare a little time to refresh yourself just when you feel like you're losing focus. This will allow you to straighten up things a little bit and regain focus. Your time is not your property but facility. Facilitate yourself in the best way possible like you would have with any other. Time would not always be nice to you, and you do not have complete control over it, but you can always endeavor to make the best of it.

Chapter 2
Failure

"Success is the result of perfection, hard work, learning from failure, loyalty, and persistence."

-Collin Powell

Failures are nothing but opportunities to redo and learn what needs not to be done to be successful. They remind us of what we tried. If we were not to try, we were never to succeed. It is inevitable not to experience failures. They are not subject to our skills or determination, but the attempts we make. It is all trial and error.

The chance of things going wrong and failing is always there, but that is not reason enough for you to not try at all. Truth be told, it is not who try that fail; it is those who do not try who are real failures. They fail to face their fears and stand in the face of reality. They fail to trust themselves and take the leap of faith to succeed ultimately. That is a failure; it is not when you do no succeed at something you try. It occurs when you do not try at all.

Failures have nothing to do with loosing. Failing does not mean losing for good. It is based on our perspective. There is a possibility that we might have failed to become whatever we had aimed for. However, if we explore different dimensions of the same situation, it would tell us a completely different story. We might not have been able to achieve our main objective but are very like to have achieved what we had not planned for. It could be patience, mitigation of losses, and, most importantly, eliminating barriers that were initially unknown.

I have experienced failure throughout my entire life. I had, by default, developed a wrong understanding of failures. There was nothing about them I could consider to be right. There was a phase in my life when I failed in every aspect. I failed to be a good father. I failed to maintain a decent financial system. I failed to be the husband a wife would ask for and even to develop a connection with God. It was failures after failures, and I still was not willing to get in terms with it. None the less I was successful in making through all those failures.

Get in terms with it

*"Failure is simply the opportunity to begin again, this time more intelligently." -**Henry Ford***

What I realized was that the first step to redirect the right approach and restart the journey through the same tracks required understanding - understanding what failures mean and that they have a purpose. No matter how accurate our calculations are, and how closely we analyze the route to success, the randomness of life overdoes it all. There will always be things we cannot know.

The storms coming our way would not necessarily give signals of their arrival. We cannot be prepared for everything, which is why failures can never be escaped. We might complete a few passages without many difficulties, but some bridges would be hard to cross. If we put an end to our journey where we fail, success would become inaccessible.

The pattern of life revolves around emotions. Our sensitivity and desires influence our decisions. Failure can be painful, and it can cause us immense discomfort and agony. If we intend to escape these emotions, we would be wasting our time and energy. This goes for every man living on this planet. You will get your share of pain, and it will have a valuable role to play in developing your personality and defining your goals only if you have the right mindset.

If we were not aware of the misery caused by pain and suffering, we would not have known the true essence of relief and happiness. If we do not fail, we are in no way to value success. Excitement would lose its energy, and we would be least concerned about it. The need to meet our ambitions would die out, which would destroy the purpose of living.

Make mistakes

"Failure is the key to success; each mistake teaches us something." -Morihei Ueshiba

The failures can be a result of the wrong choices we make. Mistakes can exceed the losses beyond our predictions and hypothesis. Our mistakes do not define us. They are everything we're not. That's why they're labeled as 'mistakes.' We can learn from them, and we can find the space to recognize the better alternatives, which at the point of making decisions did not seem logical or close to being right.

I made several mistakes throughout my life. My failures were not because of my bad luck but because of the bad choices I made. I would not have been what I am today had I not made them. I learned from them, and when I look at the magnitude of mistakes I made in the past, I only thank God. The consequences could have been far more significant, and I feel blessed to have not faced them.

We do not have to be embarrassed by our failures. They are natural. If it were not because of our choices, fate would ensure we get our share of failures. We are all destined to fall, not just once, but over and over again. Despite the alertness and sharp presence of mind, we cannot skip them. All the hurdles we closely watch, collide into one to face us so we may deal with them.

Even if we pretend we never failed, it makes us nothing but inhumane because humans do fall. I want you to know I failed in almost everything because I want you to learn from my experiences. People may judge you if you share your stories with them, and that fear might demotivate you from going public. It should be your last concern to worry about what people would say or think about you. This again is something you do not have control over, and why are you to control it anyway.

You are not the first, and you would not be the last

*"Most great people have attained their greatest success just one step beyond their greatest failure." -**Napoleon Hill***

Look around at the success stories in our societies. There's one thing we shall find in common amongst them, and that is the way they embrace their non-fulfillment. They do not try burying it, but they sell it around to the world because they know what it feels like in the moment of fall. If they would have mourned their defeats and not extracted the good out of it, they were never to become success stories.

They understand the meaning of failure, and we need to understand it too. We have to be comfortable around it. We need to confront our fears and not let them stand our way of trying. It depends on how we perceive the impacts or effects of an event. It is about the way we examine the ignored realities of the same event that has prominent de-motivations entitled to it. Successful people have a thing with failures. They are aware of the distinctive characteristics of failures, which make them go after their dreams with more conviction. They are not among the rest who start walking back rather than pushing forward. That element is complex and can vary from people to people. What is similar about it is it being the driving force to accomplish our goals. Life is a lot like its dimensions. Whether it is relationships, work, or dreams, they all require impairment. Recovery is a process that will always remain to be a part of our lives. Smart people do not get stuck in the phase of loss but jump onto the recovery phase.

We are all going to get hurt and get tested. Life is a test itself. It is about losing, tripping, and getting back up. It is about the process of recovering. Whenever I would find my life on the low, I would search for the catch in it. I would question God about what he wants me to learn from the experience. Take your failures as a trailer of the movie, which is a success.

All those movies only become interesting when there are challenges and failures in the lives of the protagonists who ultimately also succeed. This is why they display suspense-filled trailers where the lives of movie characters are in shambles, and they are failing. Remember, the results that you finally obtain do not derive from failures, but your reactions to them.

Be optimistic

"Success consists of going from failure to failure without loss of enthusiasm."-Winston Churchill

We are programmed to react to everything that happens around us. Those reactions play a critical role in setting the route to achieving our goals. We are to identify our strengths, which fuel us to move on and strive to move forward. All of this depends on self-belief, and that self-belief is subject to our solidity. Things do not always work as per our will. Our wishes are not always fulfilled. We have to fight when the odds are against us, and that requires commitment and dedication. It requires faith above all.

The first time I decided to start a business, the decisions I made were not very smart. Despite having no past business experience, I invested a huge amount of money. The sea looks different from the outside, and we only get to know about it once we get in. I was under a lot of stress, and that stress influenced my decisions to a considerable extent. However, this was not the only mistake I made. It was not long when I realized that the business was to collapse.

At first, I was not willing to accept it, which made me make more mistakes. It is indeed essential to fight if we are to succeed, but we need to make sure we are fighting for the right cause. I was only fighting to deny the failure coming my way. The moment I realized it was a battle long lost, I gave myself the courage that I will make my way through it. It was something I naturally had that kept on telling me I was to make it to the other end.

It was maybe the will to move forward or identification of a strength that was not to be explained but executed. Even if my conscious self was not able to express it, my subconscious guided me. I considered myself to be a tough guy, and if you think you are one, it is difficult to digest defeat. I had a tough time admitting to the fact that I had failed. Every night is followed by a day.

No matter how dark the night is, the dawn breaks. I was focused and was hoping to get done with the darkness and wake up to a fresher morning. I also had good friends. They were people who motivated me and guided me through times when self-belief and determination were nowhere to be found, *"You are on the floor Melvin, what worst can happen, you would not roll-off."* These words of a true friend are unforgettable. They became my strength and fuel. They had me going and confronting what I never thought I'd be able to. In the words of my role model, Les *Brown, "When you fall down in life, try and land on your back because if you can look up, you can get up."* I fought those circumstances, and in that moment of the fall, I preferred standing tall.

Great names, greater stories

*"Your attitude towards failure determines your altitude after failure." -**John C. Maxwell***

We cannot let others decide who we are to become. Our failures do not give them the license to define our lives. Imagine if you cannot speak until the age of four and receive remarks from your teacher that you would not be able to make a difference in your family, let alone the society. Then imagine that kid being Albert Einstein.

Had he not reciprocated, he would not have led the world to new scientific explorations. There was a college kid who was removed from his basketball team. The kid spent the entire night locked in his room, crying. That night was dark for him - darker than it was for the rest. He waited for the day to shine brightly upon him, and he shone like a star. He was none other than Michael Jordan. He did not let his basketball coach decide his fate. He dared to battle the crises himself instead. Walt Disney was fired from a newspaper company because they thought he had no imagination. He had terrible financial crises and went bankrupt seven times. He was so affected that his health degraded and had to face two nervous breakdowns. The world knows him as a man to have the most exceptional imagination of all times. He contradicted the tags the society had associated with him. He failed enormously, but he carried on.

Steve Jobs was removed from the company he had built. He was depressed and treated with injustice. He did not attempt suicide, nor did he believe that it was the end of the world for him. He turned out to be one of the most influential CEOs of the world. He was cheated and failed, but he had the driving force - the force, which is a pre-requisite to success.

Eminem was a drug addict and had a disturbing domestic life. He had witnessed violence and hatred from a very young age. He got addicted to drugs and was only sinking deeper day by day, yet he kept battling poverty. Had he stopped, nobody would have witnessed the greatest rapper in the world. He knew he was to fail enormous times, but he did not give up. His logic did not support his actions; his heart did. He is now a success story the world exemplifies. Thomas Alva Edison's teacher thought Edison was not good enough for science and education. He thought it would be wiser for him to work on the field as labor. Thomas did not listen to it but instead focused on his dreams.

His invention - the bulb - is unmatchable. He was given the title of 'Sir' for his valued contribution and his failure, in contrast to his success, is negligible. However, that failure is what motivated him and propelled him to do wonders. Failures are this way - they are there to make you aim for higher.

The greatest president of America had a history of failures. His fiancé, who he considered his strength, died. His business was never in good shape. He was the son of a shoemaker and was taunted to aim to become one. He fought elections one after another despite losing every time. He lost eight elections altogether, yet, he found his failures to encourage him. Today, the world acknowledges him as a great leader. There are thousands of stories, and all have failures in common. The more the number of failures, the greater is the difference they've made. We need to compare our situation to theirs. Have you lost a loved one in the process? Have you been through the worst medical and financial conditions? Have you been forced to quit on your dreams? Or do you have natural obstructions or disabilities standing your way?

Suffer-ring

"Remember your dreams and fight for them. You must know what you want from life. There is just one thing that makes your dream become impossible: the fear of failure."
-Paulo Coelho

We will only find ourselves to be lucky when we compare our struggle to theirs. If we are to quit on easier problems, what is to happen when the magnitude of problems is insanely high? Backing off on troubles is backing off to success. Every successful intellectual has a story. The story is full of suffering. They are not fairy tales, but real situations that are even unimaginable at times. All we are left with is to wonder how they made it through despite undergoing all of it. The key to it is persistence. They did not set their targets and goals with a condition to accomplish them on fixed trials or period. The attempts are not of any concern, but getting to the other end is. No matter how many times successful people fall, they pick themselves off the ground, wipe the dirt off their shoulders, and moved on. That is the thing about them; they move on in the same direction that was uneasy and full of storms. They never care what people have to say. They are willing to make tough choices. It is about how we prioritize our goals because our choices and decision are based on that prioritization.

I started taking failures as a step to success. Every failure brings you a step closer to what you want to achieve. The higher the dream is, the longer is the journey, and more are the failures we are to encounter. Success is not just connected with our ultimate goal. We want to be successful in all domains, which is why we fail in every single one. They are not synchronized.

We can be excelling in one while failing in the other. Our attention has to be distributed amongst many aspects of our life. There can be times when every element appears to be on the low. It is a very complex situation where we might feel to be hopeless. That is when we are going to need the spirit to believe in ourselves and our ambitions. We are the ones who've set them, and we are the only ones who can turn them into reality.

Conclusion

*"We all learn lessons in life. Some stick, some do not. I have always learned more from rejection and failure than from acceptance and success."-**Henry Rollins***

Every time we feel we have been through worse, the range of possibilities makes you reconsider. We can never know the worst a man can face, what we can know is that no matter how bad things seem, there is always a way of making through it. Falling is not our choice; getting up is. Every time we make an effort to regain our position, we learn of a better way of getting up. We learn another way you could fall. The learning process is constant, no matter how things proceed.

If by any means we think we're not failing at all, this is not a good sign, my friend. That only means we are not trying because of our fears or because we are not aware of our potential. Either way, what you're missing out is the urge to succeed. The first step in being successful is to train yourself not to be afraid of trying. There are going to be negative consequences sometimes, but to bring out our true self, we must take the right steps and, above all, we must keep trying. Failures are a part of life. We do not have to run away from them. Failing is the first step to reaching your goals. If we do not go through this natural process, we are least likely to be successful. That way, we can never exceed our expectations or make a difference - the difference that we could make if we did not think of failures as the end but as a new beginning.

Chapter 3
Stay Away from Negative People

"A lot of people will ignore positive words when they are down and accept negative words. Those people never get better."

-Travis J Dahnke

We all want to be happy in our lives. The definition of happiness may vary, but in the end, whatever the cause is, it is what completes us. Good and bad days take their turns. That is just how nature balances our lives. If there is no sadness, there would not be any happiness either. It is just like how light and darkness co-exist.

If you had not seen darkness, you would never appreciate the light. The case with happiness and distress is no different; the existence of one replaces the other. Every person has negative thoughts, and in no way can you ever get rid of them. Yes, you might control them or reduce their impact, but there is nothing you can do to mitigate their existence. Similarly, negative people will always be a part of life, and not always would they be eradicable. Nevertheless, successful people transform their negative energy into positive energy, redirecting their focus on becoming their best versions.

Those who are negative can harm your life in multiple ways. They can hijack your thought process and push it down the wrong road. This will be a road that does not stretch in the direction of your goals. On the other hand, there is a lot that negative people teach you, but you can only learn if you have the right mindset.

When you think of the people you know, you might identify quite a few people who serve as sources of negative energy. They are generally people who can emphasize the negative aspect of every reality, even if it does not exist. They have the talent to prove to you that it does.

You might have realized that the company of negative people is not fun, but it is not the only problem they are causing you. What goes unnoticed is the negative impact they have on you and your success. If you are still unsure of who a negative person is and why he/she is negative in the first place, this definition will simplify the idea. Negative people tend to be downbeat. They enjoy disagreeing and are always skeptical. In other words, they are people who are rooting for the worst to transpire.

Negativity is synonymous with irritability and hopelessness. Such catastrophic thinking is what leads a person into depression and anxiety. It is what makes negativity different from the ingrained disposition. More often than not, negativity causes a person to derail. It can ransack the most positive people around, so it has a lot to do with how we deal with a situation.

Vulnerable

"Surround yourself with only people who are going to lift you higher." -Oprah Winfrey

We humans are highly vulnerable. Our attitude and behavior reflect our present circumstances and distress in life. This is especially true for times when we are suffering from an illness, betrayal, job loss, or find ourselves in a state of turbulence. The probability of us being affected by the negative person becomes higher amid such events. Again, however, you can counteract negative feelings associated with these events with the right mindset.

Humans, in their low time, tend to share their pains and sorrows. The person who they confide in, however, is not necessarily somebody who cares about you or your worries. They can simply be a friend with a positive attitude who brings hope into their lives or just someone who makes you believe more trouble is headed your way.

Vulnerability is not just limited to times when we are suffering, but it could be higher in times when we are very hopeful for things to go our way. In such situations, the people who support and help us endure our hardships are keepers. On the other hand, the ones who further complicate our position are those we should be distant from.

If you are trying to be patient and do not keep away from toxic people, it might push you to a point where you begin to think that you can never fight your way back. Be with people who bring happiness to your life and inspire you. They are the ones who will encourage you and will guide you to identify your true potential.

Remember, life is too short, and you only live once. You do not want to waste most of it staying in the company of wrong, toxic people. There are lots of good people out there, and there is nothing wrong with changing your company.

You need to realize and control the damage. Once you set your intentions straight, the next thing you have to do is act per your intentions. You need to take all the necessary steps required to change your company. You will always find negative people around you, at your workplace, or even in your family. That does not mean their negativity must have an impact on you. Find a mentor, a person who can help you in dealing with the day to day affairs. Somebody who can cancel out the negative energy you receive with a positive attitude.

Set Limits

*"Beautiful things happen in your life, when you distance yourself from the negative things." -**Zig Ziglar***

As mentioned earlier, you can never just stay away from all the negative people you know. Some of them can be very closely associated, and you might as well be concerned about them. It could also be your boss, who is someone you cannot avoid for obvious reasons. There are ways that can help you defend yourself from the negativity thrown your way. Whether you are stuck with them for half a day or longer, you need to learn to deal with them before you lose more than you gain. The reason complainers are bad is that they want more people to join their complain gang and maximize the negativity of the environment. There are times when we are bound to listen to negative people. Sometimes you only do so because you do not want to seem rude by ignoring them and walking away. On other occasions, they might have good command over communication, which keeps you sucked into the conversation. There is a fine line between listening out of sympathy and getting emotionally-affected. The transition can be quicker than your realization.

The only way you can avoid it is by defining parameters. The cigarette analogy might help you understand it better. For instance, a person is sitting and smoking a cigarette. Would you prefer sitting next to him, inhaling the second-hand smoke, or would you simply avoid the environment? This is exactly how negativity works.

There is nothing wrong with distancing yourself. In all honesty, it is the best way to deal with toxic people, i.e., by not dealing with them. If the idea of setting limits appears confusing to you, let's keep it simple. When you ask a negative person what the problem is, they get frustrated. All you have to do is show your intent to fix the problem. When you do so, either the conversation ends, or the negative person begins to talk with positivity. For you, it's a win-win situation.

Pick and Choose your battles

"Negativity can only feed on negativity." -Elisabeth Kubler-Ross

It is not going to be a piece of cake, but whenever someone tries to victimize you with their negativity, learn not to engage. Arguing or drawing to a conclusion is also not a wise option. It will not only portray you as argumentative, but the toxicity will get into your own space. Instead of trying to reason with a pessimist, try avoiding the conversation by telling them that you have something important to do.

Pretending to agree, hoping that it would be your escape route, is also not the best approach. It will not only prolong the conversation but can also have a lasting impact on you. You might want to work on your emotional intelligence to ensure the situation does not escalate. You are always going to have conflicts, and taking the highway is often the wisest decision. Another thing about pessimists is that they will always try to derail you off your positive mindset. They just have so much negativity in their system that it directs them away from the subject of discussion. Not all battles are to be won. Try making your point when the other person is open to opinions; otherwise, it's nothing but a waste of your time.

Identifying a negative person

"You cannot have a positive life and a negative mind." - **Joyce Meyer**

There might be people around you that you may not have considered as negative. It might have struck you to notice how they act or behave, which is how you realize that the person you are speaking to is full of negative energy. Here are a few ways you can identify a negative person and stay away from them.

Constantly worrying

Worry is what negative people require for survival. It could be caused by the need to feel protected or something else. Whatever it is, they always find something to be worried about. People who worry about things that are beyond their control are usually identified as pessimists or negative people.

Opinions or Commands?

The people who order you to follow their commands, like telling you to change your job, what car to buy, or in other words, tell you what to make out of your life, are undisputedly negative-minded. They might not confess, but when you do a little research, you would not be surprised to see that their life issues are unresolved.

Position Unchanged

People do not become negative just like that. Science has a neurological explanation for their actions. Our brain has a part called the amygdala. This part functions as an alarm, which is continuously in search of danger or trouble to have the alarm ringing. According to scientists, it is the default position of the brain. So, naturally, the brain has neurons that are assigned the job of taking all the bad news to it. The people who do not learn to re-program the amygdala have more negative thoughts than positive ones. Positive people, on the other hand, develop an ability to deal with problems, altering the mechanism.

Secrecy

When you run into a negative person in a gathering, you will find their conversation to be very tedious. They might refrain from revealing information about themselves because they are scared of it being used against themselves one way or the other. The negativity in their mind is what makes them act this way. Whenever you feel defensive during a conversation, know that the negative energy has probably taken over all your positivity.

Pessimists

Negative people are incapable of finding a positive outcome. For them, the possibility of something worse to happen never fades away. Even if there's nothing wrong they can find, they wait for something to wrong to happen.

All they have is bad news

Negative people love breaking the bad news to you. In fact, the bad news is all they have. Every time you have a negative person come up to you, they will talk about all the terrible things that have happened. Negative information has a direct impact on a person. According to various researches, the information related to violence and tragedy leads to depression and anxiety. This is one important reason why you need to reduce the sources of negativity in your life, whether it is a person or a media channel.

Thin skin

Negative people are extremely sensitive when it comes to criticism. They might even take the compliments the wrong way. Innocent remarks can be condescending for them. For instance, a short-heighted person might find jokes about short people offensive, even when it is not linked with them. It is how the brains of negative people function.

Always Complaining

A negative person is convinced that the world is against them. They have various reasons to justify their failures. Sometimes it's the bad weather that allows them to complain, while on other occasions, they believe to have been cheated by luck. They never look at factors that explain why results are or were against their will. Since they fail to notice, they fail to learn and improve as well.

They never step out of their comfort zone

They are never willing to move outside of tested waters. They try their best to avoid any discomfort or failure. It refrains them from having new experiences. As a result, they only dwell in their dry comfort zone. Whenever you find a person scared, without knowing what they are scared about, you have most likely come across a negative person.

'But' is their go-to word

It's not that negative people are always short of compliments. They might compliment you for the food you have cooked or the dress you are wearing. They might enjoy spending time on the beach or dining at a decent restaurant. No matter how happy they might seem, they have an urge of ending their sentences on a 'but.' It is what transforms the positive statement into a negative one.

For instance, if they like the food you made, *they will say, "It is delicious but would have been even better if you marinated it for a little longer."* These were a few of the many attributes negative people have. The above factors are most commonly found in negative minded people, but these are not the only ones. Some people might possess all these traits, while others might only possess a few. It all depends on how negative the other person is.

Find your way out

"Wound is where the light enters the soul." **-Rumi**

Identifying the negative people that surround you is not enough. You have to find a way to battle your way out and ensure that their negative energy does not sabotage your life or push you away from the road to success. Negativity can only be fought with positivity, but it's definitely not as easy as it sounds.

The set of instructions given below is a simple representation of key points that shall keep you on track. You are going to need a lot of courage and clarity in the vision to act in the right manner. Like I said, reading about it is different than working on it.

Never Buy into Negativity

If you do not allow yourself to be affected by negative toxicity, you can never be victimized. Avoid speaking to those who are habitually skeptical. If you try to reason with them, it is only going to stoop you down to their level.

Always maintain an emotional difference, which is not ignoring them, but making sure you stay unaffected from their negative vibes. Any attempts to convince them are going to go in vain.

When negativity becomes part of a person's personality, altering is close to impossible. Negativity drives its nature to be demanding. In return, they transfer their internal pressure on their peers. One of the reasons as to why negative people act this way is because they have a high need for respect and love. It contradicts their own cognition process, which is against showing any emotional support toward others.

We all have our expectations, but dealing with them in the right way is very critical. In times when you are depressed, turning to a negative person is only going to increase your misery. If you are unable to avoid engaging with them, try using the noncommittal language. Just acknowledge their comments through noncommittal language. Do not endorse what they say. Although you cannot change their personality, you can balance their toxicity with your actions.

Problem Solving is Not Your Domain

Do not take it as your job to make sad people happy. If you plan on completely changing a person's life, it is going to leave you in utter disappointment. You are only responsible for your won happiness. To do so, your attitude when dealing with negative people should be very positive. Just control your thoughts and intentions from trying to change the person's life.

An easy way to annoy a negative person is by telling them to smile when they are not happy. Pessimists, in such situations, might want to hear your thoughts, but if only presented gently. The ideal approach to protect yourself from a negative person is to be confident and protect yourself by shunning away what you do not like. A negative person will make you doubt your abilities, but the final call is always yours.

Take a Break

When you set boundaries, it gives you the liberty to take a break. Everybody needs space, and so do you. When you want to clear your mind after a stressful situation, always be alert to avoid getting exposed to a negative person. Their toxicity will otherwise make you feel worse. You might be somebody who is addicted to using the cellphone. However, you are not required to check your phone in times when you need a break to revamp your thought process in the right direction. Negative people can leave you frustrated, and it is not the best time to deal with more people. Ideally, you must take some time for yourself and clear your head.

Do Not Let Your Tongue Slip

Your lousy mood after meeting a negative person is the most direct impact he/she has on you. If their negativity makes you feel uncomfortable and you decide on responding with anger, it is only going to intensify their negativity. When they realize that the victim is no longer reacting with anger, they prefer changing their target, and you enter the safe zone.

Negative people often make insensitive remarks and make direct personal attacks on the other person. It depends on how miserable they are. When they interpret reality in the wrong sense, they get aggressive without even knowing that their interpretation is wrong. A pessimist might sometimes be trying to make a valid point, so just listen to them and take out whatever positive you can from it.

Conclusion

Those with a negative mindset will always discourage you from following your dreams. "A man is known by the company he keeps," is not just a phrase. It is very close to reality. When you are surrounded by positive people, you receive a lot of positive energy that helps you staying focused and motivated.

I had a very difficult childhood myself. My stepmother was not a positive figure in my life. She always discouraged me and left my confidence shattered. When I was finally able to get away from her, I changed. I moved in with my grandparents, and a lot of things in my life transformed. I realized how much the company of a person matters. When I began living with a good company, I developed a positive attitude and began to walk down the road of success. Today, I am content with my life.

Not every person who fights with you is your enemy. Likewise, not every person that hugs you is your friend. I always tell this to my children. Stay with people who are positive, and try staying away from those who are negative.

Learn to deal with negative people as you will always run into them several times throughout your life. If you are focused on your goals, you can easily manage to learn all these traits required to be successful.

Chapter 4
Please Use Your Gifts

"To find out what one is fitted to do, and to secure an opportunity to do it, is the key to happiness."

-John Dewey

Have you ever wondered what makes diamonds precious? They are made from the same carbon that is the central component of coal. The reason diamonds are attractive is because of their value, which is complemented by their appearance. Now imagine, if you find thousands of diamonds under your possession, will you not become wealthy?

Here's the good part. You have thousands of diamonds worth millions of dollars in your possession. You just do not know. They exist everywhere around you. However, to find these precious stones around you, you shall first have to embrace their existence. If you do not believe something exists, how are you going to find it? The diamonds that we are referring to here are nothing but your talents. All talents are not of equal worth, neither are all diamonds. To know what your talents are worth, you first have to identify them. Only then can you understand how you can use your abilities to attain success. According to this diamond theory, it is pretty evident that the more valuable diamond you find, the richer you will be. You need to know your valuable and unique talents to maximize your profits. Once you identify your best talents, then all you have to do is work on increasing their value.

It is indeed common knowledge that all of us have strengths and talents. Even then, most of us do not pay the right amount of attention to them. Every single person, no matter which part of the world they reside in, is equipped with certain qualities and talents. Nonetheless, not being able to use your abilities is just equivalent to not having any ability at all. We are all liable to use these talents to improve the society we live in.

We are all special!

"We are all special cases."-Albert Camus

You might have heard that every human being is born with a set of unique talents. Every person demands attention and desires importance. It is a common attribute found in all humans. Time and again, we find people pondering over our purpose of life. At least once, usually on multiple occasions, we question our purpose and attempt to think beyond the obvious. We try to understand what uniqueness we hold and why do we hold it in the first place. Yes, we all have a specific purpose, which is directly related to our talents. The sooner you identify your talents, the sooner you find your purpose.

You may have many strengths and abilities that are reliant on your intention to explore them. In the journey of life, you are destined to have various experiences. The outcome of different experiences is meant to differ, too. Some might have lessons embedded in them, while others might be there to enlighten you about your strengths and weaknesses. To act wise, you need to learn from these experiences and use them to identify the talents you have.

It could be through any means, or the reason behind your realization can be very random. It could be through a pen, where playing with words helps you express out your uniqueness. It could be to the rhythm of the music that allows you to display your distinctive attributes, and it could be only through communications. 'How' is happens is not important to know as long as you get to learn about your skills and develop the confidence to portray them. Anything that has your flavor and emotion has a direct impact on the people around you. If you think your existence does not matter, you are entirely at fault. Every person matters because each one of us has a role to play for the betterment of society. Consider it the reason you were born for.

It is not tough to believe and realizing that everyone, including you, has a special talent. What is difficult is identifying your hidden talent. Many have a difficult time understanding the special quality they possess. Even after finding it, some people fail to understand how important it is. It might sound obvious, but it is not. Most people are unaware of the fact that the special talent they carry is connected to the purpose of their lives. It is what they are meant to do. Whenever you think that your existence or genuineness is not important for the world, revisit the statement removing 'not' from it.

Self-worth is not very easy to recognize. The biggest hurdles in this realization are our self-limiting beliefs. You might have never thought of yourself as somebody who can influence people. It could be because of your siblings, who might have outshined you in school. Also, our society might have discouraged you in a way that it made you focus on your weaknesses and not your strengths. We all have our weaknesses, but focusing on them is never a wise trade. It is one of the main reasons why people fail to identify their passions.

Remember, not recognizing them will not diminish them. They have always been there and will never leave you, regardless of whether or not you use them in the right way. However, it is evident that the more you polish them, the more valuable they become. On the contrary, leaving them untouched does not reduce their worth either.

Now that you know ...

*"Identifying and utilizing your God-given talent is your greatest chance of success in life." -**Billy Cox***

Once the idea of having an exceptional talent is no more alien to you, the next thing is figuring out what your unique ability or skill is. To start off, do not feel any shame in seeking advice from the people you know are your well-wishers. When you are prepared for the journey, you might need some navigation to ensure you are on track. The advice can serve as that navigation. You do not have to rely on it completely, but discussing it with people you trust is only going to help.

Here are a few steps that might help you in drawing out a close picture of what you truly want from life and what you shall give to it in return.

Childhood is the beginning

Childhood is that phase of our life where we do what we love doing. We are independent of any peer pressure, and since the social norms are somewhat non-existent then, the space to exhale out our desires is endless. When you are trying to understand what your true passion is, think of your childhood memories.

Think of the things that brought you joy during elementary school. Think behind the reason that made those memories memorable. When you take an in-depth look, you are most likely to find a common thread.

Pose more question at yourself. How competitive were you as a 10 - 12 year old? What was that thing at school that you enjoyed the most? Something that you lived for in that phase of your life. Something or the other must have been of your interest. The purpose of asking these questions is to identify it. Once you have found the things that you enjoyed, the next step is to relate them with something that fascinates you as an adult. If you were competitive as a child, you are most likely to have a similar mindset after growing up. It means your love for complex and strategic projects might not have faded away. The only difference will be the fact that back then, you were competing against fellow class-mats, and now you do it for a multi-national firm.

It is your unique talents that show you why your choices are different from the choices of others. You might be good at one thing, while your sibling or friend might be excelling at the other. Call it God's miracle or nature; every person is different from the other, and that is how every job in the world is being done. If all of us were capable of becoming doctors, who would teach our kids? Likewise, if all of us got white-collar jobs, who would we call to fix those leaking pipes in our homes? The chances of having the same talents and a personality when compared to anyone else is so low that you could consider the idea unrealistic. In other words, what excited you as a child, will most likely thrill you as an adult. To narrow it down, the tasks you enjoyed as a child are likely to shape your future. Believe it or not, the early-age stories can be very powerful to reveal the talents you have but have not identified.

When time loses its importance

We are so involved in our everyday affairs that we do not find any time for ourselves. For instance, think of a Sunday morning when you are entirely free. There is no soccer game you have to play or no corporate meeting that you have to attend. Your calendar is all yours for the next few hours with zero commitments.

In such a situation, what is going to be your favorite activity? Are you going to enjoy playing with the strings of a guitar, or are you going to read a book? You could even be working on the development of a software or something other less technical – anything that is going to be your product and no one else's. No matter what the activity is, if it draws your complete attention, you are enjoying it. It brings your thought process and body in total symmetry. You start at 10 in the morning and do not realize that you have been engaged in the activity for so long until you observe the time on the clock signaling its one in the afternoon. You did not even feel hungry amid the activity you were engaged in and could not think about anything else wither. Why? Because you were doing what you like doing.

Now compare it with your regular job. Was this Sunday morning way more fulfilling than your regular job? Any activity that gets you so involved that you fail to keep track of time is a sign you must pick. It tells you what you like and want as opposed to what you have been doing.

Your yearnings

Whether or not you know it, there is a fire burning inside of you. Even at this very moment while you're reading it, the fire is still burning. With advancements in technology, life has become a lot easier. Today, it would not be wrong to state that the world's socio-economic situation is very suitable to work on your dreams. For instance, if you had always wanted to be a writer, how difficult is it to start writing a blog. Just grab a paper or flip open the laptop and start shaping your creativity into words. The advent of e-commerce stores has made it a lot easier for start-ups to function and operate at a low cost. Even young teenagers today can start a business of their own, without investing a single dollar into their business. If you need more contacts and intend to expand your social circle, all you have to do is arrange for a meet-up in your city.

Idealistically, we would all want to get jobs that we enjoy. Work can never become a passion, but your passion can be what you do for a living. We all like to play around our strengths as our strengths make us who we are. Unfortunately, not everybody is lucky enough to find a job where all they have to do is use their strengths and nothing more.

At present times, most people do not have the luxury to use their natural talents at work. The ones who do excel become well-known intellectuals, while the unlucky ones spend their lives trying to learn a job, they were not born to do. Take the example of the eagle; it flies at around 100mph. What will happen if it is made to fly at a meager speed, say 10mph? It will only struggle and suffer to no gain. Humans, too, are programmed per their skills, and if they work on talents they never had, they are most likely to fail over and over again. So, whenever you feel you're in a place where your actual skills and talents are untapped, take the realization as a blessing. Instead of being demotivated and uncomfortable, think of how you can change the course of your life. What had to happen had to happen. You cannot change your past but surely can work for a better future.

The good you're missing out on ...

"Talent is an accident of genes – and a responsibility."
-Alan Rickman

Humans were made to live together in communities. Humanity circulates the idea of commensalism – the concept of two individuals benefitting from each other. It clarifies the idea that we have a social responsibility to share our talents with the people around us to improve their lives. It is the purpose of our creation.

Have you not been benefitting from others' talents? Look at the things around you. The light bulb invented by Thomas Alva Edison or Ford's automotive idea, and many others have only simplified our lives. Even the food your mom cooks for you is something that benefitted you. To sum it up, everyone around us contributes to our welfare, and likewise, we must do the same in return. Are you still thinking about how other people can benefit from us? Let's make it even simpler. We have complete ownership of the gifts and talents we have, but it has to be understood that they are not just there for us. We have them for a purpose, primarily to share it with others. Trust me, you would not want to live in a world where nobody shares their talents. In that case, the world would no longer be a place worth living.

Also, a person can never be at peace if all he/she can do with their talents is to use it for themselves. The fulfillment of sharing our talents is unmatched when compared to only using it for our own good. You get to use your talent, while the other person gets to benefit from it. This makes it a win-win situation.

Becoming Successful

Money is everyone's basic need. Our jobs and constraints are usually dependent on our financial shortcomings. If using your talents for money makes you feel guilty, stop thinking that way. Having in mind that our talents are not limited to generating cash but serve a bigger purpose is good enough to maintain balance. Of course, we can use our talents to make money as long as it is not the only purpose our skills are serving. If they are nourished and polished in the right manner, your skills can even make you a rich person. The richness might not necessarily just be seen in your financial stance but in various other aspects. Even if you are working in a different field where you are unable to explore your talents or make use of them, it's still not too late. Well, it's never too late to learn, is it? The moment you identify your talent, you can think of a way of using it for monetary gains. Even by starting small, you can climb newer horizons of success.

Most people on identifying their talents, use it as a sidekick. Eventually, they realize the potential their talents have and soon convert their part-time job into a full-time one. This is what most successful people did and claim. They first identified what they were good at, and gradually, it became the source of their success. Many opportunities are lying around us, and like mentioned earlier, technology has further eased the process. No matter what we are good at doing, there is always an opportunity waiting for us to grab it.

Leaving a legacy

To leave a profound impact on the people you meet, you shall have to showcase your talents in a way that others get to learn from it. Here's Arianna Huffington's story, which she shared in one of her books, "Thrive." The book is about her sister Agappi.

Agappi had graduated from the Royal Academy of Dramatic Art, London. As per the story, she had received multiple awards even though she initially did not get a part in a theatre play she desperately wanted. Disappointed by fate, she lost any motivation to continue working on her talents. She would have never gained success in her life if it was not for a stranger she met.

The stranger changed her way of thinking and perspective about life. Her courage to open up to a random stranger helped our look at things from a different angle. Right then, she also had the opportunity to discuss her life with a woman, who also helped her in shaping her ideas.

The lesson that women taught her on the bus ride changed her life completely. She got very confident and learned that touching others' lives and giving unconditionally was brought about the most fulfilling feeling.

Try giving somebody a present and observe their reactions while they are opening it. The feeling is amazing. Try it yourself, and you would not agree more. The feeling will make you want you to share more gifts with more people. Similarly, when we share the talents we have, we are opening up more doors for ourselves.

This is how nature works. When you give something to the world, you receive something in return -something far better than what you gave. Our talents are like investments, and if we do not capitalize on them, they shall never grow.

The first thing is to identify your talents, followed by nourishing them and finally sharing them. If you think that your talents are only for you, it is only going to serve like a reserve, which will eventually dry up. The moment you decide to help others with your skills is the moment your talents begin influencing others. You find the purpose of your life and learn to grow and excel on all grounds overcoming all obstacles lying in your way. Your success, after all, is dependent on the choices you make!

Chapter 5
Never Live in the Past

"There are far, far better things ahead than any we leave behind."

-C. S. Lewis

It would not be wrong to say that the past is no more a real thing. You cannot be in the past or change anything that has happened in it. Therefore, nothing from the past is real in the sense of its tangibility. In other words, anything that our five senses fail to register can never be a part of our lives. Now, this sure does not question the existence of them in a different time period.

It was just a phase that has passed. So, why exhaust over something that is no longer a part of your today? Millions of brain cells store almost every bit of information that has happened with us and our lives, which means the past sure exists in our psyche, but how we use that information is totally up to us. What comes to your mind when you think of the past? Some of it would be lovely memories and heart-throbbing moments that bring a smile to your face, while the others might make you regret your decisions and push you into pain and agony. Here's the interesting part – there's nothing wrong in being visited by dark memories; what's wrong is trying to erase them from your past, or think of how different they could have been. If they were to be different, they would have been different. Stop stressing over it!

Different people react differently to the memories of their past. Some of us find peace in them, while others struggle to push them away. It sure depends on the impact their past has had on their lives. The power we give to our past is what influences our present. The past demands us to stay in it, and the present is what suffers. Subsequently, the hopes of a bright future fade away. Not only do our goals lose their importance, but our relationships with our friends and family also get equally affected. Your past might have weakened your thought process and altered your behavior, but you can always revamp your cognition and set things right.

Knowing the Problem

*"We do not heal the past by dwelling there. We heal the past by living in the present."-**Marianne Williamson***

Not everyone around you lives in the past. Some of the people you may know might be contented with their present and optimistic for the future. The question here is what makes the two different.

A lot of it has to do with our environment. When you live around people who constantly blame their past for their shortcomings or losses, you also subconsciously learn to put it on the past whenever things do not fall in line with your expectations. It could even be possible that a person might have inherited specific kinds of genetics from their family. Things like depression and anxiety can also lead a person to dwell in the past.

One of the most common reasons a person prefers living in the past is because it can act as a coping mechanism to escape the present. It helps you avoid the responsibilities you should take of your happiness and your life. The blame game is the easiest to draw to conclusions, and what better way could be there than blaming something that is unreal – not tangible. Another key factor often overlooked is the low level of self-esteem. Not all, but many develop a psyche that they do not deserve to be happy, just because they have done something they should not have. Self-sabotage is what leads them to be stuck in the past. For instance, an unfortunate event transpired in your life might constantly make you feel like a victim.

When you constantly replay those disturbing memories, it gets all the more difficult for you to get past it. There can be many other reasons that make your past a safe zone or an area you are unable to get out of, but the moment you realize the chains of the past are not permanent and can be broken is the moment you begin to see the change.

It's not just you who suffers...

"Living in the past is a dull and lonely business; looking back strains the neck muscles, causes you to bump into people not going your way." **-Edna Ferber**

Living in the past is not only harmful to you, but it equally affects other people around you. As mentioned earlier, what suffers the most is the relationships. Take the example of a child who lives with a father who is always saddened over things that had happened over the past. No matter what the reason behind the sorrow might be, when a child finds a parent dwelling into the dark valleys of the past, he unwantedly and unknowingly follows his parent.

Even though the child may not share a similar past, but living with a person who never stops mourning over the past, the child cannot help it but develop a similar trait. The same could be the case with the better half of your life. The victim never stops feeling ignored. He or she feels to be taken advantage of or, even worse, might have a feeling of being invisible. As the river of time keeps on flowing, the person staying with you moves away with the water, as you keep staying there like a stone, unmoved. Eventually, it creates a gap between you and the other person - a void that often remains unfilled.

The ones you might love the most might be the ones who get the most neglected. These are all consequences of living in the past. Even if the other person tries to help you, living in the past will lead you to ignore him/her, and gradually the hopes of recovering will keep getting lower. The bond you have with the people around you is jeopardized when all your attention is centered toward the past. The present is what should have your attention. However, with the past dominating your mind, you just do not mourn over the dead past, but also kill the present moment of liveliness.

Coming Back to Life

*"Every moment you live in the past is a moment you waste in the present." -**Tony Robbins***

The past can never be changed, so any attempts of you trying to change it are only going to go in vain. Even if it makes you feel miserable, you will have to learn to walk out of it. When you realize coming back to the present is the only solution to any problems affiliated to your past, the equation loses its complexity. If you consider yourself as a person who is addicted to the past, the supply of your past memories makes it even more difficult for you to come out of it. Hence, it's time to get clean. Here are a few things you need to tell yourself to start living in the present.

Step 1 - The way you take your miseries

It's not that the recollections of the events that have happened in recent or not so recent times do not benefit us in any manner. The case is similar for most habits we possess. Maybe the bad outdoes the good, but that's not the point we're trying to make here. Like every other habit, living in the past also has some of its benefits. All we need to understand is what we are losing in the process.

You might be wondering what good does come along with dwelling on the past. For the ones who still have not been able to figure out what we are implying to here, it's not that complicated to understand. Basically, it gives you control. Not everyone is profound about happiness. Quite a number of people know what fulfillment truly is, in fact, the concept is a little too scary for them. Fearing instability is somewhat natural, and that is where preferring to stay in the past comes into play. It gives you a sense of control when everything around us is chaotic. It is what prevents us from being vulnerable. It is about coming in terms with your misery. It is certain and, like every unrealistic entity, can be controlled in accordance with your likings.

Moreover, some people even use the miseries of their past to get distracted from the present. The reason behind it could be a feeling of emptiness, or it could be the fear of exhibiting courage. They can also be the ones who are afraid of their own failures or can be victims of existential crises. If you want to avoid any responsibility you have, spending time with your miseries is the easiest way to avoid them.

Step 2 – Knowing what happens if you ignore your miseries.

Since we know dwelling in the past has some benefits associated with it, we now need to understand how different things are going to be in their absence. Before reading any further, establish this as a fact that if you are totally honest to yourself, your miseries are going nowhere.

So you could either be dwelling on the past to flee away from your responsibilities or have total control.

It could even be the memory of a loved one who is no longer by your side, their absence making life far more disturbing than you had expected. Whatever the reason is, imagine what happens when you get rid of it. Is there something that you lose? If so, what is it? Like it or not, it's only you who knows the answer, as that 'something' is different for everyone.

After identifying what you are most likely to lose, think of what happens when you surrender to it. If you find yourself in the position to move on, you sure have moved on from the past, and the future ahead of you is brighter than ever.

Step 3 – Engaging yourself.

We all need diversions to drag our attention from one aspect of our lives to another. When you engage yourself in something else, you give yourself the leverage to look at things beyond your past. It is about replacing being engaged in the past with something in the present. The ideal thing for you would be getting involved in something you were always passionate about. Otherwise, it would not be easy getting involved in something that does not really interest you.

It does not have to be something far-fetched, as it could be something as simple as writing your own book, working on a personal project, or even cleaning the house. Do not judge your interests, and just do whatever you feel like doing. If you are not sure what could be a good thing to remain engaged in, start thinking about it. The process itself is a form of being occupied. If there are many things that keep you busy in the current moment, staying in the past will no longer be possible for you.

Step 4 – Being Thankful

One of the biggest setbacks of living in the past is that it prevents us from valuing the present. To be thankful for the things we have, we must know what we have and what we do not. Once you realize that there are plenty of things around you that deserve your appreciation, you would not disagree that having a sense of thankfulness is nothing less than a blessing. Even if you do not have it yet, it does not mean you never can. The more you work on it, the stronger it will become.

When you begin cherishing the things you have and develop the idea of contentment, you learn that it is indeed quite helpful to get distant from the habit of being consumed by things that have already happened. Take it this way, whenever you feel like you need to spend some time in the past, ask yourself, what is it you have that needs your appreciation and gratitude?

Step 5 – Life is and will always be uncertain

Nothing about life is certain - be it the bigger prospects or the little ones. Sooner or later, every person realizes that life is a tale of uncertainties, out of which some are cherished, and others are not. In that moment of realization, we often find peace in the past. When the reality is far more disturbing than the past, living in the past is what brings us comfort. Although the feeling serves as a temporary relief, we still prefer investing our time in it.

Losses and failures are inevitable, but they are not a bad thing. In fact, they are the only things that provide us with strength and help us grow. If it was not for our failures and losses, we would not have become wiser and stronger in many ways.

It sounds a lot simpler to be consumed in the past, but it is truly a lot more complex than how it sounds. Coming in terms with the fact that the past is dead and shall never return or change is one thing, but replacing the negative mindset with the positive one is an entirely different thing. The only time you should look in the past is to learn from the mistakes you've made. If you get stuck into it, you fail to progress in life.

Conclusion

The past is like a catalog that only has things you had. Every passing second can never return. Good and bad times in life take constant turns, but the bad ones are more tempting to cling on to. Call it human nature or modern human psyche; complexity is what attracts us. We look for peace in the wrong places and wonder why it is so hard to be happy.

Always remember, whether its good times or heart-wrenching memories, none of it is going to return. If you try to distribute your attention equally to the two, you are working for a lost cause. Can you sail in two boats at a time? Do not make your survival a struggle by trying to do things that are not going to benefit you in a definite way. Do not prefer temporary relief over long-term distress. Learn to live in the moment, as it is the only way you can write the latter pages of your past handsomely.

At this very moment, look at what hour the clock is showing and promise yourself that from now on, you are not going to get stuck in the past. Use your past as a guide to battle difficult situations, not as an escape to avoid them. You might have suffered losses that can never be made up for, so stop hoping for any recovery. You might have lost loved ones that can never be replaced, but in the process, do not lose the ones you already have.

The first step to setting things right is knowing what's wrong. You might not have noticed how affected you were from living in the past, and it's fine to have spent some time in the wrong direction. However, now that you know you were walking down the wrong road turn around and embrace your present. It is how you will learn to embrace happiness.

Chapter 6
Freedom of Letting Go!

"The more you let go, the faster you will move ahead."

-Alan Cohen

It is easier to say, but to let go is not that simple after all. All our lives, we are taught to hold onto things, situations, opportunities, and whatnot. Often, grabbing and clinging on is not the wisest thing to do. It is in those times when you have to learn to let go. If you do not learn it when you're young, it will be a lot difficult for you to understand it in the latter phase of your life.

To let go is to release dead leaves that no more have any life in them. If you are expecting it to be a smooth and effortless process, it is going to be far more difficult for you than you anticipate. Remember, we're letting go, opening doors for freedom and self-control. Since when did freedom start to come without a cost? Our youth is the most happening phase of our life. We are full of energy, willing to experience anything and everything.

My youth was no different than that of the average kids of my age. I was struggling to make a mark, unable to excel in any field. It was a critical time of my life, and that was when I wrote a letter for the 21-year-old me. Today, I dedicate this letter to all youngsters and hope it helps them hold onto their strengths and let go of their weaknesses. I hope it opens up doors to a new world, just as it did for me.

Dear Melvin,

I know you're going through difficult times. You're new to the journey of life. You were walking with your parents and guardians throughout your childhood, but now, at this very moment, the driving wheel is under your command. The excitement of independence has begun to fade away as the horrors of the darkness ahead captivate your imagination. Before pushing the gas paddle any further, I want you to take a pause, sit back, and restructure your approach.

It is nice to see you are concerned about the future, but what worries me is over-concern. Dwelling in the past and thinking of the future is consuming your present. Learn to live in the moment, as it is what matters the most. What has happened cannot be unchanged. What the future holds will always be a mystery. The present is your most honest friend, and its time you start treating it with respect. It's about time you start living in the moment.

The past cannot be fixed, so you are directing your energy toward a lost cause. Would it not be better if you use this energy for a bigger purpose - the purpose of achieving your goals? You are meant to do great things, but how are you to walk down the path of success if you lack self-believe. It is you who needs to know what you're capable of. The past might discourage you or draw your attention toward it, but you will need to take control of the situation and look ahead instead of looking behind.

You may or may not be responsible for all the losses you incur. Others could be the reason behind your failures, but there is no point in holding onto those failures. Forgive others because that is the only way you can put your past behind you. Forgiveness is essential for progress. You are God's child, and the only thing standing between you and your success is "you."

We are all meant to make mistakes, but the wise ones learn from the mistakes they make. Help others love God and not a particular religion. Spread the message of love as what you spread is what comes back to you. Enlighten others with the fact that love is not a condition. It is something you must always have. Then, the world will be nothing more than a playground, where if you work hard, success will become inevitable.

In times when you feel sad, just remember, bad times will never stay with you forever. Melvin, I want you to know that no matter how difficult things appear and how horrific the reality might sound, nothing lasts forever. Just like how happiness does not stay forever, neither does pain nor agony. The waves of time, like the waves of the ocean, never return empty-handed. Every wave takes with it some grains of sand, some pebbles, and pearls. The pearls are things that make you happy, and the pebbles are events that are unfortunate to have happened. If the waves do not hit the corniche, how are they to take the pebbles away? In the process, some pearls are meant to be lost. The grains of sand are abundant, but for the sea – the sea of time, so are pebbles and pearls. You are not the only person standing by the shore waiting for the waves to bring newer and better realities along with it. Similarly, not a single man standing at the beach leave from there in disappointment.

I hope this leads you to a new beginning.

Simple Steps

"Surrender to what is. Let go of what was. Have faith in what will be." -Sonia Riccoti

If you want to develop the trait of letting go, there is nobody besides you who can help you accomplish it. You'll need to do some hard work, and here are a few tips that will help you to stay on track and equip you with the spirit of cutting lose and letting go.

What is most important to you?

The first thing is to take a step back and determine things in your life which are of most importance to you. Once you begin to think in that direction, you would not be surprised to notice that a lot of the things you thought were important, actually are not. Now the next question is, what is important for you?

When you realize that you had given importance to the wrong things, you learn the things that require your attention. Things like health, positivity, mindfulness, and most essentially living life to its fullest. The list might have more things than mentioned above. Holding onto things and even people for that matter is a sign of no progress. It means you still have not begun experiencing true freedom. Your belief system is holding you from striving forward. So the first step is to realize.

What is that you're truly gaining?

More often than not, we cling onto people and things only because we believe that they add value to our lives. The illusion that we are benefitting from them is what keeps us from thinking in a different direction. When you think of it, you might not be on the benefiting end. That is because to go for change is a lot more complicated than settling down with the present. When you reflect on how a particular person or thing is not adding value to your life, letting go of them becomes a whole lot easier. It sure does not mean that you should only hold onto things that benefit you, but what if you're giving a lot more than you're receiving? What it still be the right thing to hold on? Of course, not.

You might be overvaluing a lot.

Think about it. Is there a person or thing which you consider to be of high value? Is it the reason you're holding on to them. Now, is the value you've given way more than what the person or thing deserves? Unknowingly, on plenty of occasions, we begin to idealize people and decide that having them out of our lives is out of the question. You stay trapped in a situation that is not meant to benefit you in any manner, all because you falsely believe it will. In such situations, you might hear a faint voice coming from inside you telling you to let go. Listen to it and learn to let go. Otherwise, you will continue to suffer. There will be another voice in your head telling you to over-value, it's the voice you're not supposed to listen. Letting go is the tougher choice, but it is the one that will help you excel.

The strength you have is the strength you need.

In the end, it all comes down to the ability to let go. It is not going to be easy. The more you think of letting go, the more obstacles you might find lying in your path of success. As humans, we prefer taking the easy way out, and that is often what leads us to failures. Experiencing freedom is your choice, and you will have to be brave to stand up for your decision. It is the only way you can get rid of unwanted things, which are slowing you down and keeping you distant from your goal. It is about doing a favor to yourself. It might appear to be very difficult, which it is, but when you reap the fruit of the right decision you've made, you sure would not have any regrets.

Conclusion

"Letting go gives us freedom, and freedom is the only condition for happiness." -Nhat Hanh

While you are learning to let go, you need to know what's best for you. The instinctive feeling of doing something is of far more important than we think of it to be. There will be plenty of occasions when you hear a voice in your head asking you to let go. Do not ignore it. The voice is only heard when you are doing something wrong with your life. You sure will hear it when you're forcing yourself to do something against your nature to please somebody whom you have wrongly overvalued.

The voice disappears when you try connecting with people who work to bring out the best of you. It is nowhere to be found when you do things that draw you closer to your success. Yes, it's hard to ignore the voices in your head, but sometimes, it's even harder not to obey them. It's like knowing what is right yet not doing it for some vague reason. The vagueness fuels the voice, and consider yourself lucky if obeying it is easier for you than ignoring it. The longer you take to let go after realizing you're holding onto the wrong ends, the more difficult the process is going to become. Take inspiration from the trees that effortlessly get rid of leaves that are of no good any longer. Letting go is meant to be tough, like all good things in life. Keep telling yourself that the pain will go away as the fresher leaves will soon grow on the branches, making the tree of your life more beautiful than it ever was.

Chapter 7
Do Not Talk to Yourself
Out of Your Greatness

"You can keep talking yourself out of the thing you're hoping for, or you can decide that your dream is more powerful than your excuse."

-Rachel Hollis

You're not the first person who has had ideas of doing something unorthodox. Many greats have passed before you, and many greats will follow. Thinking out of the box is not a trait you alone have, nor is it something you are not equipped with. You might have limited resources, or something more important might be happening in your life, but none of it should barricade you from reaching out to success. What would you be using if Bill Gates thought he lacked the potential of building the operating system the world is going gaga over? Think about it! His professors never thought he would excel; in fact, he was a college dropout.

It was not just the voice in his head that was pouring negativity into his life, but even the people around him. He was just one amongst the many who learned to handle every bit of negativity heading their way. Yes, people like Gates are highly passionate, but passion alone is not what gets you through; commitment does.

Back to the question, would you be using an operating system as amazing as iOS is if Bill Gates had fallen prey to negative thoughts infesting his mind? The answer is yes. Wondering how and why? Because opportunities do not wait for anyone. They keep moving around until they find someone who can cash them. If Bill Gates did not, somebody else would have made it into the list of greats in place of him.

The difference between successful and unsuccessful people is their attitude. Think of other names; Steve Jobs, Warren Buffet, Martin Luther King, Albert Einstein, and so on, and reflect on the life stories of a few. Whether or not this fact surprises you, none of those whose names we glorify today and respect had a smooth past. In fact, they faced more hardships than the average man.

The All-Powerful "Self-Talk"

*"Instead of talking yourself out of your future, start talking yourself into it." -**Joel Osteen***

Never underestimate the discussions you have with yourself. Thinking is a characteristic of the wise. The inner voices in your head are nothing but your thought process. There are times when you feel positive about everything happening around you, and then there are times when nothing seems right. The voices in your head have a direct relation to your present and past. If your past has not been in accordance with your likings, it sure does not mean your future has to take a similar route. It's you who decides and not the voices in your head.

Nevertheless, being successful is not just about ignoring the voices you hear, because in doing so, you might lose any opportunity to improve yourself. Nobody's perfect, and neither are you, so the voices are not going to be completely wrong. They kind of have their biases, which are more dependent on your attitude and experiences. Change the approach in which you listen to what your brain has to say and feed it with more positivity. Things do not change overnight, but if you are headed in the right direction, you'll make it to your destination sooner or later. On the other hand, some people tend to consider the voices in their head useless. Fighting negativity is not about ignoring it, but is about listening to them and staying prepared for the consequences or possibilities. Listen to every word that your mind has to say to you and then ask yourself what can be done to make things better. If you are committed to doing something, difficulties will never put you to a halt. What you should rather care about is how you are going to overcome them.

Stop Now!!!

Instead of talking yourself out of it by hoping that nothing negative will happen if you fail, focus on building your confidence to deal with the consequences." -Dr. Theo Tsaousides

The first thing you need to do is cognitive restructuring. Generally, this is a technique practiced by therapists, but on a basic level, you can use it as a self-help tool. It is basically the identification of a pattern of your negative thoughts. Once you figure out the pattern, tampering such thoughts becomes a whole lot easier. The brain is the control unit

(CU) of your body. The idea is to feed commands in your CU that generate automated responses whenever negative thoughts grip your cognition. Does not make sense? Keep reading! Whether a person seeks professional help or decides to bring change on their own, cognitive structuring is a step-by-step process. You first identify the problem in your thoughts. Next, you evaluate the problem, and as per the evaluation, you replace it appropriately.

It is just like going to an automobile mechanic. They first carry out a diagnosis to spot the problem. Then they evaluate the problem deeply to understand the extent of malfunction to conclude which part has to be replaced. The machinery of your brain can always have an excess of toxic thoughts, which you yourself will have to assess and rectify.

Initially, when you acquire this approach, you might have trouble keeping up with the newly adopted mindset. With time, however, it is not going to seem as complex as it does now. You are training your brain to develop positivity and pay attention to rational thoughts only. Once the brain is trained, you would not have to put in any effort as it will generate positive thoughts on its own. You are just reprogramming the brain to ensure it serves you best.

In a state of Assertive Defense

*"Figuring out what you can't do is not 'being realistic.' It's just talking yourself out of going for the better life you want to live." -**Doe Zantamata***

People will always be judgmental of you, and the criticism coming your way is not always going to be constructive. Most of the time, it is only going to make you feel uncomfortable, sabotaging your self-esteem, and cause you to underestimate your self-worth. When you fail to cope up with rejection, you often end up being a victim of your own thoughts. The criticism of the other person is not what impacts us, but the way we take that criticism is what matters.

In all totality, being mindful is what keeps you in a state of assertive defense. It is a state in which you ensure that any negativity coming your way either through your thoughts or other people around you does not push you to a point where you become hopeless. For the ones who have not been in such situations might have a hard time believing it. Trust me, though, when you are finding a hard time in maintaining a positive attitude, nothing in life seems right – not even the things which really are right.

Being mindful is learning to objectify your feelings in the sense that it is you who decide what you want to hold onto and what you want to let go. It is to gain total control of the reactions caused by fluctuations in your emotional behavior. Your brain should no more be a battleground for thoughts that are of no benefit to you in any way.

Do not mistake mindfulness for thought-stopping; the two are complete opposites. Thought stopping is a process in which your brain works like a radar. What you identify is negative thoughts, and you work on eliminating them without paying any attention to them. The problem with it is that the more you try to block and filter out negative thoughts, the more they approach you. Allow those thoughts to come in and analyze them in-depth. Take all the positive out from them, and ignore anything that is of no use. Be mindful of your thoughts.

Conclusion

"The way to get started is to quit talking and begin doing." -Walt Disney

We all have the potential to do wonders. You are special and not just in a single way. If the plans you make or the vision you have seems farsighted and difficult to accomplish, that in no way means you need to change your plans. The more difficult it appears, the more phenomenal the results will be. The reason we become prey to the voices in our heads is that we naturally prefer choosing the easier route. Remember, giving up is always easier. Always listen to the inner voices in your head, but be prepared to respond to them. When the voices tell you that you cannot do something, you answer them how it can be done. When the voices tell you that you are too weak to see your dreams accomplish, tell them you're ready to walk the path and see it yourself.

When you decide to work on your dreams, be prepared for severe opposition and criticism from the world. Your inner conversations have to be strong to walk past all that people have to say and chase your dreams and goals. I recommend that you come up with a daily regimen to combat the negative voices that you have within your mind and also what the outside voice, i.e., those of the world, say. You do this regimen at least three times a day. I can almost guarantee once you have a positive routine set for your mind, you will start to see the change.

For so long, I let my inner conversation steer me down the wrong path. Once I realized that there was no enemy on the inside that could hurt me, I knew that there was no enemy on the outside that could hurt me either. We become our own worst enemy with the inner 'negative' conversations that we have about ourselves.

I often wonder how many great ideas were lost because individuals have talked themselves out of tremendous opportunities in their lives by having negative inner conversations. Do not waste your life talking yourself out of your dream. Be passionate, tenacious, and confident about the conversations you have with yourself. You are a product of your thinking. Just think positive and act on it.

Chapter 8
Breaking Points

Have you ever found yourself in a position where you feel you have lost the strength to take it anymore? In all honesty, we have all been there. Even then, the words spoken are interpreted differently by different people. Quite understandably, though, as our experiences are unique, so are our strengths and weaknesses.

It is a fact that there comes the point in every person's life, which they consider to be their breaking point. Yes, we reach our breaking point in different ways, and it has a lot to do with our personalities. For instance, a person who is continuously pressurized might not respond even a bit. Similarly, somebody else might simmer and explode. It is all based on how we relate to stress as the breaking point is the point when we fail to cop up with excessive stress.

Stress is a very common word, but most of us haven't pondered over our stress response in depth. Reaching the breaking point is not a sudden process, but a gradual progression. To understand it better, I have divided it into three levels or stages. The first stage is when you admit to the fact that you are under pressure, but the feeling of being in control hasn't left you. The second level is when you begin realizing that the pressure and stress are exhausting you both emotionally and mentally. The key here is to avoid any anger on anxiety-ridden reactions.

The third stage is when you think you cannot take it any longer. It could be referred to as the moment of an outburst. At that moment, if you fail to hold onto your emotions and frustration, it leads you to do things that you regret later. With that said, embarrassment is not all that matters, but fighting your breaking point is. If you don't do it wisely, you are more likely to do it the other way.

Chronic stress builds up over time. It is the opposite of acute stress, which happens at once, such as someone facing a car accident or the demise of a loved one. We all deal with chronic and acute stress differently, and so do our hormones. To cope up with chronic is generally very difficult all because you have been ignoring it first, and usually admittance hits you at a point when you find yourself at a low point your life.

It is often the people and not the things

Humans are always going to be the cause of pain and agony in one's life experiences. Not always do others around you have ill intentions, but then again, not always are their intentions pure and honest. It is people who soothe your heart and its people who cause trouble to it.

Early in your life, it is one of the most important lessons for you to learn to make friends with the right people. When you stay with people who constantly test your patience and keep pushing you to your limit, it leaves you in a state of despair. The continuous urge to rise from below, alters the idea of success in your mind. You tend to leave your ideas of success behind, striving to meet people's expectations without even knowing how sincere they are to your cause.

I must accept and be thankful to God for always being amongst people who were sincere to me. Remember, it is not situations that drag you to your breaking point, but the people involved in it. Your company can make life miserable for you, just as how it can help you walk through difficult situations. Would you invest in a business that does not have the potential to prosper or help you grow in any way? Then why think differently when it comes to the people you spend time with? My idea of people and how they affect your life is not just pointless theories but is a reflection of my experiences and the lessons I have learned throughout life. There were times when I had to visit the court regularly, trying to prove my innocence. Financial instability was an integral part of my early life, and it was a battle that wasn't easy fighting. When you have the basic necessities of life, you tend to misinterpret the idea of stress.

What you see on the outside is nothing when compared to what isn't apparent. My grandparents had a vital role to play in explaining to me and helping me understand the true meaning of honest relationships. They guided me through my early life, ensuring I did not take a destructive route. Life is not always as pleasant as you want it to be; in fact, it is never nice to you when you expect it to be.

More often than not, I was put in a position where I felt I couldn't take it anymore. I wanted to kill the people who betrayed me in times when I was at my lowest, but then I had sincere friends around me who helped me not break when everything about life was suggesting otherwise. And for that, I shall be forever grateful. True friends never judge you. They try and understand your situation and help you in making the right decisions. Like I said earlier, it is people who make you go through worse, and it is people who help you get through it. You just have to identify the ones who are on your side, and then you are good to face any storm heading your way.

Stay Prepared!

Would you walk with your shoe for days if it had a rock in it? Of course, you wouldn't. You would stop the very moment you find something bothering your foot. Life is a series of events that happen as per and against your will. Sometimes your work relationship will make life difficult for you, while on other occasions, it could be a loved one acting up.

The only time I can guarantee you that no stress will walk your way is when your breathing gives up on you. Since stress and life get along too well, even exceeding our likings, avoiding it is closing your eyes on it. The wisest thing to do here is to have a rebuttal for your problems and never allow the thoughts of other people to control your actions. Trying to put up with stress and assuming your breaking point can never grow big on you are both mistakes we don't realize while making. The effects are not only evident in your everyday life, but even at a physiological level. If you can't change the situation, why stress over it? On the other hand, you will always be in a position to change the people you spent most of your time with. It might not always be the case, but it is more likely to be the case most of the time. Learn to stay distant from people who bring negativity and stress into your life. The moment you learn to do so, half of your problem is resolved.

The first person whose help is most required is yourself. It is your mind that decides the winning side. In other words, victory and defeat are nothing but mind games. Others around you can be of great help as the support they provide you is indeed quite helpful. The key is the game played inside your mind. Your emotional reactions are what decide your fate, and if you fail to react wisely, things are most likely to go downhill.

Believe it or not, fighting the unknown is very much human. The human minds love to stay in charge, and that is why breaking points are all the more difficult to handle. The desire to be in control hits the randomness of the situation, shattering you emotionally. Learn to tell yourself that not always will you be in control, and in times when you can't be, learn to surrender. Not all battles are worth winning. With time, you'll learn to identify the ones which are.

Conclusion

If you think you have no breaking point, you are probably too young, and there is a lot you have to experience. Everybody has a breaking point, and it is something you learn with maturity. As humans, we are always going to need help. There is no harm in seeking help in times when you feel on the low side. You must look for help in the right places, but what is even more important is to understand that wanting help is not your weakness, but a human need.

If I did not look for help, things might have been a lot different. I might still be failing to get beyond my breaking point, and success would have been a mere fantasy for me. The same will be the case for you if you do not understand how important it is to consult people that you trust. We all face breaking points in our life. Although there is nothing we like about challenging moments and trying times in life, they are what define us.

Prevention is undoubtedly the best medicine, but not always can you be successful in doing so. Whenever you find yourself in a tough situation, never hesitate to count on people you trust. Learn to control your mind and accept the fact that you can't always have things your way. Every now and then, you might find yourself combating against your breaking point; what matters is how you grow and groom yourself. It is what distinguishes successful people from unsuccessful ones.

Chapter 9
Don't Get Lazy!

"Tomorrow is the only day in the year that appeals to a lazy man."

-Jimmy Lyons

Laziness is not a very complex term, and we all know what it implies. It is when a person fails to do something that they had intended to do just because of the effort required to complete the task. Even if the activity is carried out in a perfunctory manner, it is influenced by laziness.

As humans, we have a natural tendency to be attracted toward something that is less strenuous or boring, when compared to the task at hand. There are times when the lack of interest leads us to remain idle, while on other occasions, we search for reasons to excuse ourselves. No matter what approach we acquire, laziness does not benefit us in any

way and is indeed a term that has a negative notion. For instance, if you Google the word and search for its synonyms, you wouldn't and shouldn't even be surprised to find words like sloth and indolence in the list. Now, if we further get into understanding what they mean, we get to know that all of them refer to taking the easy route. There is no harm in going with options that requires less effort, but what matters is what we trade off in the process. More often than not, the consequences of laziness work against us, instead of ever working in our favor.

Not everybody attracted to laziness is innately lazy. Other reasons include lacking the idea to pull off a job or finding a better basis for not doing it. Sometimes motivation is all that we require. It is a fundamental lesson in psychology that since our childhood, the concept of reward and punishment trains us to opt for a job. As we grow older and begin to gain control of the decisions we make, we learn to take the effortless route.

Laziness is what attracts us the most. It is indeed a very critical stage of our life, as it is a make and break situation. If we get addicted to laziness, it usually stays with us for the rest of our lives. While, if we learn to avoid it for obvious reasons, the characteristic of managing it somewhat becomes our strength. Other than the apparent reasons of purposelessness, laziness can also be a product of hopelessness driven by some specific kinds of fears varying from person to person. The fears could sound absurd, like the fear of being successful or the lack of self-believe. Although success, unlike laziness, has a positive notion, it still can cause people with low self-esteem to not work for it. It is the only thing that encourages them to work against their goals. On the other hand, another reason why people prefer laziness is because of the fear of failures. They just don't put in the effort fearing to not benefit from them.

Similarly, hopelessness can affect the ability of people to think through problems. Hopelessness simply implies believing that things cannot happen any differently. The idea can be so staunch at times that it can fail us from thinking of a solution. For anybody who prefers to choose laziness must know that despite how soothing it seems in the moment, the long term effects are never satisfying. Although it is difficult to categorize people as lazy or hopeless, the negativity associated with both these terms is what makes them a lot similar.

Here are a few drills that might help you to fight laziness and walk the road of success.

Being too overwhelmed

*"Laziness is nothing more than the habit of resting before you get tired." -**Jules Renard***

There are times when there is just so much to take care of that you prefer doing nothing at all. It can get difficult for a person with so much work at hand to figure out where to start. Sometimes, the reason behind it is overestimating our capability or having extremely high expectations. Nevertheless, you will have to start off somewhere, lower your expectations, and start working. Even if you can't have it all done, at least strike out the things that you can.

Motivation Check

*"Laziness is a secret ingredient that goes into failure. But it's only kept a secret from the person who fails." -**Robert Half***

Motivation is the key source of your strengths, encouraging you to ignore laziness completely. Being productive is directly proportional to laziness. It can be tricky for you to remain connected with your motivations. There could be multiple things you intend to see through, or the problems surrounding you might make you think in a different direction. Whenever any such thing happens, remind yourself of what is important to you and find the motivation.

Look around you

"Only laziness and apathy make us hate life." -Leo Tolstoy

The environment we live in and the people we remain surrounded around are of great importance. Gradually, or abruptly, we are definitely to take influence from their presence. It isn't us who decide whether the influence is going to be a positive or a negative one, but our company. For instance, if most of your time is spent with people who are always complaining, you are to end up like them. Similarly, if the people with you are always motivated to strive hard and never sit back, you are to be one of them and grow just like they do- learning at every step.

Valuing Time

"Indolence is a delightful but distressing state. We must be doing something to be happy." -William Hazlitt

Time is money, and it isn't the first instance you're reading it in this book. Laziness is the parasite that directly eats away your time. In today's world, there are plenty of things that help us do nothing at all. We can spend hours and days doing nothing in particular. Once you realize the importance of time, the next thing you have to do is plan it. Instead of meeting deadlines in your head – as it is never going to be of any use – start writing things down. If you don't prioritize your goals, nobody else will do it for you.

The Right Mindset

"The idle man does not know what is to enjoy rest."-
Albert Einstein

The mindset of considering "work" unhealthy and "play" worth doing is not going to help you in any manner. It is precisely the mindset of a young school kid, who is yet to understand the purpose of life. If doing something is a punishment for you, then the state of success would replicate hell in that regard. You don't want to drive to failures. If this is the problem with you. Constantly keep informing yourself of the positives affiliated to your work. When you experience the satisfaction of accomplishing something significant, you won't fail to find the positives in working and the negatives of wasting time.

Refresh your Habits

"A life of leisure and a life of laziness are two different things."-Benjamin Franklin

Usually, we keep the most difficult tasks for the last. Even while attending a math exam, we first attempt questions, which we are more confident in answering. However, life is a lot more complicated than a math test. Often, when we keep difficult tasks for the last, they stay unattended, and all we face is the consequences of not doing them.

If you are amongst those who face a similar problem, it's time you reverse this habit. Try starting with something difficult, and keep the easier tasks for the latter. It will also give you the motivation to work hard and get done with complex tasks so that you can take care of the easier ones.

Keep Track of Your Progress

"Some folks look so buy doing nothing that they seem indispensable." -Kin Hubbard

Although committing to create new habits is one thing and literally developing them is another. When you think you are on the right track and have changed as a person, nothing else can confirm it besides the progress you have made. There is a possibility that you got rid of laziness along the way, but failed to adopt the right approach to achieve what you want or better your life. When you measure how much your changed habits have helped you get closer to your success, it not only adds to your motivation but also asserts to the fact that change is achievable.

Conclusion

Even if you have a genie with a magic lamp, nothing can change anything for you unless you yourself change as a person. If you are somebody who is always content with how things simply because working style suffices your needs, you will lack the reason and motivation to change. To be fair, in this scenario, change isn't for you. Change is for the ones who yearn to find a way to become successful. One of the main things that keep us from marching toward our goals is fear. You'll have to overcome your fear and bring change from within.

When I first moved to Texas, I worked as a real estate agent. I was young at that time and did not really know how much laziness could affect me. It wasn't the only source of my downfall, but if I hadn't been lazy, things could have been a lot different. Long story short, I trusted the wrong people and ended up spending thirty-eight days in prison. Even though I was proven guilty, I still had to face some difficult times. It was then that I realized how important it was to be active and fully aware. Laziness is not my excuse but, in fact, my mistake.

No one can ever be successful if they fail to manage laziness smartly. It includes being actively aware of the people you work and live with, along with being mindful of what you truly want at heart.

Do not look for a simple solution for being lazy. You will have to reshape the way you think and work hard to overcome your weaknesses. I mean, you can't be lazy in getting rid of laziness. Start off with self-discipline, and other things will too fall into place.

Chapter 10
Self Confidence

"Because one believes in oneself, one doesn't try to convince others. Because one is content with oneself, one doesn't need others' approval. Because one accepts oneself, the whole world accepts him or her."

-Lao Tzu

Happiness and self-confidence are deeply connected. In other words, when you have confidence in yourself, you are happy and satisfied with doing whatever the job you have at hand. All these elements are pieces of the puzzle of success. Even if one of them is missing, the puzzle is to remain incomplete.

Once you find confidence in yourself and your abilities, your energy and motivation levels set new boundaries. Achieving your goals no longer seems impossible. It is why self-confidence, in a way, is similar to self-efficacy. They are both focused on the future. In light of how psychologists define the two terms, self-efficacy emphasizes the ability of a person concerning specific interests and tasks. Self-confidence, on the other hand, is a broader term catering to a person's perception of their overall capability. Believing in yourself gives you the liberty to step out of your comfort zone and explore your skills by trying new things. It helps you to enjoy challenges instead of fearing them. For instance, when you want to accomplish something, the first thing to do is putting yourself out there — something which you cannot do with a lack of self-confidence.

Confidence allows you to devote resources to the task at hand rightly. It is what saves you from wasting both your time and energy, worrying that you aren't good enough. The energy is directed in the right direction, thus enabling you to perform better. With a low confidence level and self- doubt, even the things which you can do, might become impossible to do.

Take the simplest example of making a presentation. If you are confident about what you are going to present, your complete focus will lie in delivering the appropriate message. You will ensure your audience is engaged and buys most of what you share with them. However, the absence of confidence will be opposite to it. The fear of not being paid attention at or the nervousness of not being able to communicate will dominate your thought process. It will lead you to stutter and lose concentration. Eventually, you will consider yourself a bad presenter. That is how self-confidence can make a difference.

Now, the best thing about self-confidence is that it can be improved. It isn't a chronic problem that you can never get rid of. With the right approach, you can overcome your lack of self-confidence, whether related to something specific or in general.

Say No to Comparison

"You are the only person on earth who can use your ability." -Zig Ziglar

Comparison, in most cases, is not healthy, regardless of which side you are on. By 'side,' I mean the better side, or the weaker one. Think of it yourself. How do you feel when you compare your income with your friends? If your income is less than that of your friend, you might feel jealous. If it's more, you might be hit by a sense of pride. The same is the case with other things when brought into comparison. Even if you conduct a basic online survey or research on the subject of comparison, you wouldn't be surprised to find negativity associated with it. Don't be surprised to read in your research that envy and self-worth don't go together. So in a way, you again have to choose one side. Comparisons can cause anyone to envy others around them. Naturally, the more envied a person feels, the more they start belittling their own self. The vicious cycle can only end if envy is taken out of the equation.

Try testing it out. Spare a moment and compare what you have with what your friend has. Even if you only focus on the basics, you might find a sense of resentment against the other person. When you think in the direction of what others have, and you don't, you will feel your confidence sabotaged. So whenever the thought of comparison jumps in your mind, just tell yourself that what you're doing is never going to be of any help to you. Life is a race, where you are not competing against anybody else, but yourself.

Self-compassion is the way to go

"With the realization of one's own potential and self-confidence in one's ability, one can build a better world." - **Dalai Lama**

What comes to your mind when you hear the word self-compassion? It has quite a simple meaning; to treat yourself with kindness. Humans are meant to make mistakes. There is no harm in being on the wrong end of an argument or job. What is wrong is to treat yourself harshly.

Mistreating yourself is never going to help you in any manner. It is in no way going to get you motivated. As a matter of fact, it is going to work completely against you. Through self-compassion, you can fuel your confidence and focus on the reasons which are to help you excel in life. All you have to do is redirect your approach. When you make a mistake, instead of being mad at yourself, tell yourself its fine, and you will be more responsible in the future. Whining over something that has already happened is only going to make you feel miserable.

Cut some slack, find reasons to laugh, and keep reminding yourself that everything happens for a reason and that like every other man who has lived on this planet, you too are not perfect. Such ideas will infuse confidence in your thought process, allowing you to work for a better future rather than wasting your energy over the unwanted results of the past.

Self-doubt is to be embraced

"You have to expect things of yourself before you can do them." -Michael Jordan

Sometimes we take too long just waiting. We are waiting for the right time to do something, and usually, we fail to identify what the best time was. There might have been times when you wouldn't have applied for a job, just because you thought you weren't prepared. Opportunities don't wait on you, and it's only wise to walk to them. The ones who keep waiting for a better time – a time might as well never come – they lose any chance of making most of the moment.

Embracing self-doubt brings you in a position where you can face your fears. The fear of failing for some people is the deepest fear they have. Nobody wants to mess up, but not doing something just because you believe you will make a mess of it, is not the way to go.

In no way does this mean that you should avoid preparing yourself for the occasion or stop practicing for improvement. Just don't keep practicing to the extent that the opportunity gets past you while you are too busy perfecting yourself. Do whatever you need to increase your confidence, but also keep track of time. Waiting for your confidence to be overwhelmingly satisfying can be a wait that never gets over. At point or other, we all struggle with confidence issues. What we should never allow is the lack of confidence to barricade our personal or professional life. There can be various reasons that aid in diminishing our confidence, but the first thing you need to do is embrace the fact that you have low confidence issues. To rectify the problem, you first have to identify it. There is a possibility that your problem is not a lack of self-confidence but excessive of it. Life is a tale of maintaining balance, and the moment you are on either side of the weighing scale beside the center, failures are to follow you.

Along with focusing on the aforementioned traits, there are a few more things you need to work on to ensure your self-confidence isn't a hurdle, but a tool. What tops the list is your body language and how you present yourself. If you don't have enough confidence, the other person doesn't have to know it. It is your problem, and you know how to best deal with it. An act as simple as pulling your shoulders back is sufficient to show that confidence isn't your problem. There are simple tricks that can help you show how full of confidence you are, but remember that isn't the core problem. The central problem lies in having a low confidence level, and solving it should be your prime focus.

Conclusion

Having self-confidence and believing in oneself is so very important. If you don't have any confidence in yourself, how can you expect the rest of the world to have confidence in you? Self-confidence is something we are born with, which means that we are the cause of being low on confidence. If having it was your fault, resolving it is your responsibility too.

I truly believe that without self-confidence, mediocrity is all that waits for you. Self-confidence and success go hand-in-hand. It is why confident people don't really get along well with those who are not so confident. Subsequently, people who lack confidence always find confident people arrogant and condescending.

I don't understand how it can be hard for a human to be low on confidence. As God has said it, he has created us human beings in the image of greatness. Thinking any less of ourselves is like going against the words of God. Since an early age, I have loved being surrounded by confident people. Trust me; it's contagious. I remember once going to a Mercedes-Benz dealership. The salesman was so confident and full of energy that I ended up purchasing two cars that day. What the salesman told me was very inspiring. He said, "I don't sell cars; I sell dreams." It is what confidence does; it draws the attention of other people toward you.

There are thousands of examples around you. Look at Mohammed Ali; the man exuded greatness. His confidence level was so high that it was what took him off the charts. He literally spoke his self into greatness. Confident people are always exciting to have around. I look at entertainers like Chris Rock, Eddie Murphy Dave Chappelle and Richard Pryor.

When these guys take the stage, the confidence that they have is so contagious you have no other choice but to stand up and applaud. Isaac Newton said, "Energy is never lost; it's just merely transferred." Maybe the energy radiated through confidence is transferred the same way. Believe in yourself and success will follow you wherever you go.

Chapter 11
God Will Never Let You Down

"Trusting God is the answer. He will never let you down."

-Larry Burkett

Throughout my life, whenever I found myself in trouble, God has always been there to save me. He has his own ways of compensating for our losses, and just because we don't see it that way, doesn't mean help hasn't come our way. In one way or the other, if we place our trust in God, we are to win.

Pains, sorrows, and troubles are always going to meet you. Whether we like them or not, they are an integral part of our life. What joy would happiness bring to your heart, if you haven't had the taste of sorrows? What excitement is light going to add to your life, if you have never been surrounded in darkness? It's all part and parcel of life, and one thing complements the other in ways, which we often fail to understand. When one door closes, plenty of others open. It's not wise to weep over the closed door but to walk toward the opened one. God has always been there for me. My life would have been a total mess if it wasn't for His support. It's not that I am a very religious person, and I say so with regret, but despite that, God's blessings have never failed me once. Having confidence in him is what has helped me endure all sorrows and survive unpleasing circumstances. I believe that God is always there for all of us. All we have to do is ask for help. If you do so with complete sincerity, not once shall you have any disappointment.

If it wasn't for God's help, we would have never been able to rise after our falls. No matter what He takes away from us, there is always a reason behind it. It might not be apparent at the moment, but in the long run, it ends up being in our favor, not once, but always. Everything happens for a reason is not just a phrase but a reality. The rough times are there to make us stronger.

God is the All-Knowing, and He sees what we can't. He can see moments of joy, and when tears are part of our reality. He knows the intentions and situations of other people, and we are no one to judge anybody. No matter what happens to you in life, never blame the people around you.

Just have faith in God, and things will eventually fall into place. It is not always easy to accept things the way they are-especially in times when everything around you seems to be in chaos. Some events are very disturbing, and so are some pains intense than the others. It is in such situations that we have a difficult time accepting things the way they are. Just keep reminding yourself that God does everything for a reason, and even if we can't see it then, it is undoubtedly going to benefit us in various ways.

My Testimony

*"Contentment is God's way of complimenting you. Hopelessness is His punishment."-**Melvin Bethea***

This is my greatest testimony. I'm not a deeply religious man, but I have such a powerful relationship with God no other person on earth can understand. If I must tell the truth, it's nobody else's business.

God made a covenant with me before I was even born. He knew who I was before he created me in my mother's stomach. He knew my strength and my weaknesses. I believe in my heart and soul that one has to have a relationship with a higher being. Nothing happens by accident, and I strongly believe that everything happens for a reason. I have had a lot of ups and downs in life. I've had a lot of people to turn their back on me. The one thing that stayed consistent is the love of God. God has a plan for my life and yours too. No matter how much I may fight it, he will ultimately do things his way.

God watched me kick and fight for so many years and go through so many trials and tribulations, disappointments. He allowed my foolish pride to get in the way. I wondered how and why God still loved me. He showed me so much mercy, grace, and tolerance. I don't believe in luck; I believe God blesses all of us.

I wrote a chapter in this book called breaking points. It is about the point in your life when you see no hope and no light at the end of the tunnel. That's when God steps into your life and shows you the light. He has always been there for me through all my trials and tribulations. Without God's grace and mercy, I'm sure I would either be in the penitentiary, dead or mentally out of my mind. I thank my grandfather Clarence Thomas, who showed me the power of prayers. My parents introduced me to religion, but my grandfather enlightened me with the art of praying.

I remember watching him pray from the time I was three until he died. No matter how much he ran on the street, drank, or smoked, he never quit praying. Before climbing into bed, I would always see him get on his knees and pray to God. I believe that prayer is an essential part of every human's life. It is what distinguishes us from the animals. Prayer takes you to an extremely high place. The relationship of worship and prayer that you and God share is sacred. Nobody else has to be around when you are speaking with your creator.

Once you develop the habit of praying, you can feel God's power running through you. I understand now that I showed up on the planet with all the tools that are needed for survival. There's nothing any person can give or take away from me without God's permission. I know now that I can have anything in my life by just mentioning my savior's name. Amen!

MELVIN ANTHONY BETHEA

www.ingramcontent.com/pod-product-compliance
Lightning Source LLC
Chambersburg PA
CBHW032122020726
47494CB00007BA/2199